JAMES STEVENSON

Wilfred the Rat

GREENWILLOW BOOKS
A DIVISION OF
WILLIAM MORROW & COMPANY, INC.
NEW YORK

Copyright © 1977 by James Stevenson
Inquiries should be addressed to
Greenwillow Books, 105 Madison Avenue,
New York, N.Y. 10016.

Printed in the United States of America

Designed by Ava Weiss

10   9   8   7   6   5   4   3   2   1

Library of Congress
Cataloging in Publication Data
Stevenson, James (date)
Wilfred the rat.
Summary: A lonely rat is befriended
by a chipmunk and squirrel at an
amusement park and when his fortunes
change he must decide how important
that friendship is.
[1. Friendship—Fiction.   2.
Animals—Fiction]   I.   Title.
PZ7.S84748Wi   [E]   77-1091
ISBN 0-688-80103-X
ISBN 0-688-84103-1 lib. bdg.

Wilfred had been on the road for a long time. He was
hungry and cold, and snow was beginning to fall again.
He didn't know where he was headed—he only hoped it
would be better than where he had been.
The sky got darker, and the wind blew snow in his eyes.
When night came, Wilfred stopped. He leaned against
a highway sign. He shivered, and went to sleep, and
dreamed he was being chased again by big dogs.

In the morning he walked through a village where all the stores were shut, and he came to the water.

Wilfred sat down on a bench by the water. Nobody was around. Even the houses in the distance were closed. "This takes the cake for lonely," said Wilfred.

When night came, he walked away from the windy beach. A police car was driving down the road toward him.
"Oh-oh," said Wilfred. "Here comes trouble."

Wilfred ducked through a hole in the fence,
and the police car went past.
"Looks like some big amusement park," he said.
At the back of a building he found a window
that wasn't locked, and he climbed in.
It was very dark inside.

There was a room full of bags and boards and junk.
It seemed sort of cozy, so Wilfred settled down on
some sacks that were lumpy but not hard. When
he moved, they made a soft crunchy noise.
"A stroke of luck—finding this place," said Wilfred,
listening to the wind wailing outside and rattling the
window. He shifted around until he was comfortable.
"Not bad at all," he said.
And then he went to sleep.

"Good morning," said a voice.

"Hello," said another voice.

Wilfred sat up. It was daytime. A chipmunk and a squirrel were looking at him.

"Hi," said Wilfred. "I hope I'm not intruding. I was just passing through."

"Welcome to Pleasure Beach Amusement Park," said the squirrel. "My name's Dwayne." He was wearing a T-shirt that said PLEASURE BEACH.

"I'm Ruppert," said the chipmunk.

"We hang out around here."

"My name's Wilfred," said Wilfred. "Say, what
  are the chances for some breakfast?"
"You're standing on it, pal," said Dwayne.
  Wilfred looked down. The sack he had slept on
  said QUALITY PEANUTS.
"Oh, wow!" said Wilfred.

Wilfred ate peanuts until he was stuffed.
  Then Dwayne said, "Want to see the sights?"
"Sure," said Wilfred.
"Follow us," said Ruppert.

"This is fantastic," said Wilfred.

"And it's all ours," said Dwayne, "until June."

"It must be even better when the rides start and the
people come," said Wilfred.

"That's when we leave," said Ruppert.

"Leave?" said Wilfred. "Just when it gets exciting?"

"Don't worry about it now," said Dwayne. "Let's have a good time while we can."

Dwayne and Ruppert took Wilfred everywhere—
on top of the rides, under the rides, wherever there
was something to see. They came to the miniature
golf course.

"You like golf?" asked Dwayne.

"I don't know," said Wilfred.

"Let's give it a whirl," said Ruppert.

"How about some baseball next?" said Dwayne, after
the golf.
"Sounds good," said Wilfred.
Dwayne and Ruppert showed Wilfred how to crawl
into the building where they could throw baseballs.
They knocked down lots of dolls and bottles,
then crawled into the next building for a fast
ride on the wheel of fortune.

Then they went outdoors
and scared each other
at the haunted castle.

They played hide-and-seek through dark buildings with funny rides, and then they ate their lunch of peanuts in the bumper cars.

After lunch they slid
down the ice on the giant slide.
That night Wilfred said, "I never had such an exciting
day in my life."
"It was kind of average for us," said Dwayne.
"Glad you enjoyed it, pal," said Ruppert.
And they all went to sleep.
Every day was exciting and different. Wilfred had never
dreamed he could have so much fun.

One night after dinner they went over to the merry-go-round, and Dwayne and Ruppert played beautiful tunes on the melodeon. Then they walked back under the stars.

At bedtime Wilfred climbed into a big glass jar
where he'd made a bed of canvas.
"Good night," said Ruppert.
"Good night," said Dwayne.
It was quiet.
I never had a friend before, said Wilfred to himself.
Now suddenly I've got two. He yawned.
"Amazing," he said aloud.
"What?" said Ruppert.
"Nothing," said Wilfred.
Soon they were all asleep.

During the next few weeks men came and put up signs,
strung lights, and made all the rides ready to go.
"It's time to think about leaving this place," said Dwayne.
"Why do you have to go?" asked Wilfred.
"Too dangerous around here. Mr. Marble, the owner,
hates animals. He thinks we make a mess,"
said Dwayne.
"And he has a big scary dog named Mars," said Ruppert.
"Mars hunts for animals—and is he fast!"

One afternoon Wilfred found Dwayne and
Ruppert packing.
"We're getting out of here," said Dwayne.
"Park opens tonight."
"But don't you want to see—" Wilfred began.
"Shh!" said Ruppert. "It's Mr. Marble and Mars!"
They looked out the window at the owner and his dog.
Wilfred shuddered.
"We're going to the pizza place in the village," said
Dwayne. "We sleep on the roof during the summer.
You coming with us?"
"Gee," said Wilfred. "I really want to see
the park open tonight."
"Okay," said Dwayne.
"But be careful, Wilfred."
"Good luck, pal," said
Ruppert. And then
they were gone.

That night Wilfred watched all the people
arrive. The rides were brightly lit, and
there was lots of noise and music.
"I'm glad I stayed to see this," said Wilfred.

Suddenly he heard a growl.
It was Mars! Wilfred took off. He ran this way and that,
but every time he looked back, Mars was getting closer.

He ran to the roller coaster and started to climb.
Wilfred climbed to the top of the roller coaster
and stopped to rest. But when he looked around,
he saw Mars coming up the track from one side and
Mr. Marble riding a coaster car from the other.
There was only one thing to do.

Wilfred jumped!
He went down
and down
and
down . . .

. . . and landed in
a big pail of popcorn!

When Wilfred woke up, everybody was clapping
and cheering, "Hooray for the rat!"
Mr. Marble was smiling and pretending it was
just an act.
"Don't you love our daredevil rat?" he said.

Mars told Wilfred that Mr. Marble wanted to hire him
to jump off the roller coaster into the popcorn every
night. "You'll get a swell room, all the cheese you can
eat, and you'll be a big star!"

"I will?" said Wilfred. "Oh boy!" Then he thought about
Dwayne and Ruppert.

"Can my friends stay here, too?" he asked.

"What friends?" said Mars.

"Oh, a nice chipmunk and a nice squirrel."

"Not a chance," growled Mars. "No animals!"

Wilfred said he'd have to think it over.

Wilfred walked around the park. It took me a long, long
time to find Dwayne and Ruppert, he thought.
It wouldn't be any fun being a star unless they were
around, too.
He walked some more.
In fact, he said, I miss them already.

An hour later Wilfred was at the pizza shop.
"Dwayne?" he called. "Ruppert?"
"Hey, Wilfred!" called Dwayne, peering
over the roof.
"Hi, Wilf!" called Ruppert. "How was it?"
"Okay," said Wilfred. "But I think I'll
stay with you guys."
"Come on up the drainpipe in back,"
called Dwayne.
"We're having pizza!"

The next morning Dwayne and Ruppert showed him all around the village. They ran over the rooftops.

They explored everywhere. They ate a picnic on the beach and went wading.

Then they found a toy sailboat,
so they pushed it into the water
and went for a sail.

Every day they did different things, all summer long,
and every night before they went to sleep they sat on the
roof of the pizza shop, watching the lights of the amusement park and listening to the music.

"It won't be long before the summer's over,"
said Dwayne one night. "Then it's back
to the good old park!"
"For the whole winter!" said Ruppert.
"The three of us," said Wilfred.
"Right!" said Ruppert and Dwayne.